DRACULA

D1635571

RETOLD BY PAULINE FRANCIS

Published by Evans Brothers Limited
2A Portman Mansions
Chiltern Street
London W1U 6NR

© Evans Brothers Limited 2002
First published 2002

Printed in Hong Kong

British Library Cataloguing in Publication data.
Francis, Pauline
        Dracula. – (Fast track classics)
        1. Dracula, Count (Fictitious character) - Juvenile fiction
        2. Vampires - Juvenile fiction 3. Gothic novels 4. children's
        stories
        I. Title II. Stoker, Bram, 1847–1912
        823.9'14 [J]
        ISBN 0237524015

VISIT OUR WEBSITE
www.evansbooks.co.uk
Evans

DRACULA

Introduction

Abraham ("Bram") Stoker was born in Dublin, Ireland, in November, 1847. After a long childhood illness, he went to school, then to the University of Dublin where he studied mathematics. Bram then became a civil servant like his father, but he had already become very interested in the theatre. He wrote theatre reviews for a magazine and later, some short stories.

In 1878, his friend, the actor Henry Irving, appointed Bram as the manager of a theatre in London. In the same year, Bram got married.

In 1897, *Dracula* was published. It was so popular that a cheap paperback edition was published three years later.

The story of *Dracula* is unusual because it is told only through the diaries and letters of the main characters – except Count Dracula! They tell a shocking story – how Count Dracula, a vampire, comes to England searching for more victims who will become vampires, too, when he has bitten them.

The *Dracula* legend has been made into many films, including the recent "Bram Stoker's Dracula."

Bram Stoker continued writing until his death in 1912.

CHAPTER ONE

Jonathan Harker's Diary: Castle Dracula

4 MAY Castle Dracula, Transylvania

It was past midnight when my carriage turned into the gates of Castle Dracula. No lights shone from its windows. A tall old man, dressed from head to foot in black, met me at the door.

"I am Count Dracula," he said, holding out his hand. "Welcome to my house, Mr Harker."

I shook the Count's hand and shivered. His hand was as cold as ice, like the hand of a dead man. But Count Dracula's welcome was so warm that I began to feel less afraid.

"I have no reason to fear him," I told myself firmly. "He has invited me here because I am the solicitor helping him to buy a house in London!"

As I ate by the fire, I looked more closely at the Count.

His face was very pale with eyebrows so bushy that they almost met over the top of his nose. His mouth, half-hidden by his moustache, was cruel, and strange, sharp teeth stuck out from thin lips. His ears were very pale and pointed.

Suddenly, I caught sight of Count Dracula's hands as he leaned towards me in the firelight. His nails were long and pointed and there were black hairs sprouting from the palm of his hands! I shuddered as I caught the terrible smell of his breath.

8 MAY

How I wish that I had never come to this strange place!

This morning, I was shaving in front of the mirror when Count Dracula came into my room and put his hand on my shoulder. I was so surprised that I cut my chin. Why hadn't I seen his reflection in the mirror?

I turned round to look for a sticking-plaster. When the Count saw the blood on my face, he suddenly tried to grab my throat. As I stepped back in surprise, his hand caught the crucifix I wear around my neck. He became quiet once again and left me.

I went down to have breakfast, still trembling.

Afterwards, I longed for some fresh air and I decided to take a walk. But every window and door was locked.

Castle Dracula is a prison, and I am its prisoner!

12 MAY

This evening, after dark, I went for a walk on the castle ramparts. It gave me a sense of freedom to look down at the beauty of the countryside. I saw a light below me and I realised that I was standing above the Count's bedroom.

I leaned over and saw the Count's head and arms coming out from the window. I thought it was a trick of the moonlight because his body followed. I nearly shouted out in horror and disgust! I could not believe what I was seeing! He began to crawl down the castle walls, with his black cloak spreading out behind him like giant wings. He moved quickly, like a lizard.

What sort of man is he?

I am terrified, and I feel there is no escape for me.

16 MAY

My terror is growing hour by hour. Something has just happened that is so horrible that I pray that I have dreamed it all!

During my walks, I have discovered an empty room in an old part of the castle. Last night, I fell asleep there. In the moonlight, I saw three women. They cast no shadows on the floor as they came up to me, showing their brilliant white teeth.

One of them came closer than the others and I felt her teeth brush against my throat. Suddenly, I opened my eyes and saw Count Dracula. His eyes were bright red and blazing with anger as he pulled the woman away from me.

As I stared in horror, they all disappeared, although they opened none of the doors. They seemed to fade away into the rays of the moonlight. And then I fainted.

18 MAY

I am completely in the Count's power. He has asked me to write a letter to England, telling them that I will be leaving Castle Dracula at the end of June.

I do not believe him. Will I ever see my dearest Mina again?

I must try to escape.

25 JUNE

This morning, I tried to escape again – without success. I only discovered something even more horrible.

I crept into the Count's room after he had gone out and opened another door in the corner of his room. I went through it, down a flight of stone steps into a dark tunnel. It led to an old ruined chapel. There I found fifty wooden coffins, full of earth.

I took a deep breath and started to open them. In the third box lay Count Dracula! His eyes were open but he did not seem to breathe. I ran away in horror, back to my own room.

I am waiting to die.

29 JUNE

As I went to bed, I heard a whispering outside my door.

"Go back! Go back!" the Count was saying. "Tomorrow night, he will be yours!"

I ran to the door and opened it. There stood the three women, smiling and licking their lips.

What do they want? Are they going to kill me?

30 JUNE

It is the last day of June! This is the day I am supposed to be leaving Castle Dracula, but I know I shall die today…

I decided to try to escape one last time. I went back to the Count's coffin to search for keys. When I took off the lid, I saw something which filled me with horror. Count Dracula was lying there, blood trickling from the corner of his mouth.

Count Dracula was a vampire! How I hated him! And this was the creature who was going to move to London, where he would feed for centuries on blood, and widen his circle of vampires.

I could not allow such a monster to live. I picked up a shovel and hit him. His terrible head turned and his blazing red eyes stared straight at me. The lid dropped over him and hid him from my sight.

I ran to hide. Not long afterwards, I could hear the boxes being moved. And later, from my window, I saw them being taken away on a cart.

I am now alone with those evil women – Count Dracula's vampires. I shall try again to escape before night falls, before they wake up and come looking for me. I shall try to climb down the castle walls.

CHAPTER TWO

Mina Murray's Journal: Terror in Yorkshire

24 JULY Whitby, Yorkshire

This is a delightful spot to be spending a holiday with my dear friend Lucy and her mother. Already we have found a favourite place to walk - in the churchyard next to the ruins of Whitby Abbey. From there, we can look down on the town and its harbour.

It has taken my mind off Jonathan. It is weeks since he left England to see Count Dracula but I have had no letter from him since he arrived at Castle Dracula.

26 JULY

I am even more worried now about Jonathan. He has sent me a letter, dated the end of June, saying that he was leaving Castle Dracula the next day. That was almost a month ago. Where is he?

I am also worried about dear Lucy. She has started to walk in her sleep. Her mother has told me to lock the bedroom door.

6 AUGUST

Lucy is very restless. It may be because of a storm gathering on the horizon – the clouds are piled up like giant rocks. There is a Russian ship out to sea, struggling to get into the harbour.

8 AUGUST

We have seen the greatest storm on record for Whitby. To add to the danger, a thicksea-mist drifted inland. The sky trembled under the roar of thunder, the sea was as high as a mountain. The Russian ship managed to get into port, but it was empty – except for a dead man tied to its steering wheel. When the ship touched the edge of the harbour, people saw an enormous dog jump from it. Then it ran towards the cliffs, disappearing into the darkness. What a strange story!

The ship is said to contain a cargo of fifty boxes for an address in London.

11 AUGUST

It is three o' clock in the morning, but I must write about these strange events because I am too anxious to sleep. I fell asleep just after eleven o' clock last night, but woke up two hours later. I was afraid. Lucy was not there.

I ran downstairs and searched everywhere for her. As the clock struck one, I ran into the street and looked up at our favourite seat in the churchyard. As the clouds cleared, I saw a narrow band of light moving through the churchyard. And there, on the seat, was a figure in a white nightdress, leaning back. Another cloud passed over the moon just then, but I am sure that I saw a black shape bend over the white one.

I ran all the way to the Abbey. I called, "Lucy! Lucy!" and something raised its head and looked at me with red, gleaming eyes. Lucy did not answer. I ran into the churchyard, up to the seat, and found Lucy alone. She was asleep, but breathing heavily.

I quickly fastened my shawl around her. I must have pricked her throat with the safety-pin because when she was in bed, I noticed two points, like pin-pricks on her neck. There was a spot of blood on her nightdress.

14 AUGUST

As we left our seat near the Abbey, just as the sun was setting, Lucy behaved very strangely. Her face became dreamy as she looked back. I am sure there was a black shape sitting there.

"His red eyes again!" Lucy whispered. "They are just the same."

17 AUGUST

Lucy is not well. Her face is deadly pale and she seems weak. At night, I hear her gasping for air. I keep the bedroom door locked every night, and fasten the key to my wrist. Tonight, I found her leaning out of the open window. I noticed that the tiny pricks on her neck had not healed – they seem larger than before.

19 AUGUST

At last! There is news of Jonathan from a hospital in Budapest! He arrived there six weeks ago by train. He is still too ill to travel any further and I am going out to be with him.

24 AUGUST

I am with Jonathan at last. He is so weak and thin that I hardly recognised him. He does not remember anything that has happened to him. He talks only about ghosts and demons and blood. He has had a terrible shock, I can see that.

He remembers that he has written a diary and he knows that a terrible secret is in it. But he does not want me to read it. He wants to forget what has happened and start his life again now. For that reason, we are to marry this afternoon.

CHAPTER THREE

Dr Seward's Diary: The Curse of the Vampire

31 AUGUST

Arthur Holmwood, who is to marry Lucy Westenra at the end of September, has asked me to see her. She is not well.

2 SEPTEMBER

I saw Lucy Westenra yesterday. I could not find any signs of any illness, but I was not happy with her appearance. She has changed a great deal since our last meeting. She is very pale and her breathing is sometimes harsh and difficult. She complains of troubled dreams, which terrify her, but she cannot remember them in the morning.

I have written to my friend, Professor Van Helsing, in Holland, asking him to see Lucy at once. He knows more about unusual diseases than anybody else in the world.

3 SEPTEMBER

Van Helsing has been and gone. He, too, is worried about Lucy.

"She has lost a great deal of blood," he told me. "This may be a matter of life and death."

7 SEPTEMBER

Lucy's symptoms are worse. Van Helsing has come back. We were shocked when we saw her today. She was as white as chalk. Even her lips and gums were white. The bones of her face stood out prominently. Lucy did not have the strength to move or to speak.

"She will die if we do not give her blood now!" he said.

Arthur arrived as we spoke and he agreed to give Lucy some of his blood.

Van Helsing performed the blood transfusion well and quickly. Life came back into Lucy's cheeks. But during this time, the black ribbon that Lucy had started to wear around her throat slipped. I heard Van Helsing gasp as he stared at the red marks on her neck. When Lucy was sleeping at last, I mentioned it to him.

"What do you make of that mark on her throat?" I asked.

"I can make nothing of it," he answered, "not yet. But I want you to stay with Miss Westenra all night. She must not be left alone. I shall come back as soon as possible. Then we may begin."

"What do you mean?" I asked in surprise.

"We shall see," he said as he hurried out.

10 SEPTEMBER

I have been watching Lucy for the last two nights. She had no bad dreams and the colour came back into her cheeks. She was almost like her old self again. I was so tired last night that she made me promise to lie on the sofa outside her room. I did as she asked, and fell at once into a deep sleep.

A hand on my shoulder woke me up this morning.

"And how is our patient?" the Professor asked.

"Well, when she left me," I told him.

We went into Lucy's room together. As I pulled up the blind, my friend gasped in horror and pointed to the bed, his face ashen. My legs trembled. There on the bed lay poor Lucy, paler than ever. Her gums seemed to have shrunk back from her teeth.

"Her heart is beating," the Professor shouted, "but very weakly. We must give her more blood, now!"

11 SEPTEMBER

Lucy was much better after her second transfusion. Just as I arrived to visit her, a big parcel from abroad arrived addressed to the Professor. Inside was an enormous bunch of flowers.

"These are for you, Miss Lucy," he said. "But they are not to play with. I shall make a garland from them, one to hang at your window, and the other to wear around your neck when you sleep."

Lucy picked up the flowers, smelled them and wrinkled her nose.

"Garlic!" she said in disgust.

Van Helsing's face became very serious.

"Do not joke, Miss," he said sternly. "This is for your own good."

I watched my friend in surprise. He rubbed the garlic flowers over the windows, the doors, the fireplace – everywhere. When Lucy was ready for bed, he fixed a garland of garlic around her neck.

"Do not take it off," he told her. "Do not open your window or your door. Promise?"

"I promise," Lucy said.

13 SEPTEMBER

The Professor and I visited Lucy this morning. Her mother told us that she was still asleep.

"Ah, my treatment is working!" the Professor cried.

"You cannot take all the credit," Lucy's mother said. "I went in when she was asleep. The room smelled dreadful. It was the flowers, I think. I opened the window to let in some fresh air."

The Professor's face had turned grey as he listened. When Lucy's mother had gone, he sobbed like a child. Then we ran up to Lucy's room. This time, the Professor did not gasp as he saw Lucy lying pale on her bed.

"Just as I expected!" he muttered.

And without another word, he started to transfuse blood into her veins. After another hour, Lucy woke up fresh and bright and none the worse for her terrible ordeal.

What was happening? I knew that the Professor would only tell me when he was ready. He returned to Holland, leaving me to watch and wait.

And a box of fresh garlic arrived every day for Lucy.

18 SEPTEMBER

I received this telegram from Holland, twenty-two hours late:

17 September

John – do not fail to watch over Miss Westenra tonight. Very important. Do not fail. I am on my way.

Professor Van Helsing.

I rushed to the Westenra house at once, meeting the Professor on the front doorstep. The house was silent. Nobody answered the doorbell.

"I am afraid we may be too late!" the Professor said.

CHAPTER FOUR

Dr Seward's Diary: The Death of Lucy

18 SEPTEMBER

We forced our way into the house and found four servants unconscious in the kitchen. When we came to Lucy's room, we opened the door, hands trembling.

How can I begin to describe what we saw? On the bed lay two women – Lucy and her mother. Her mother had a look of terror on her face and she wore Lucy's flowers around her neck. Lucy's bare neck showed two little wounds. The Professor hurried over to them. Mrs Westenra was dead. Then he listened to Lucy's heart.

"She's just breathing!" he shouted. "But she will die within the hour without blood."

Lucy remained unconscious as we battled to save her life. When the transfusion of blood was over, the Professor handed me a sheet of paper that had fallen from Lucy's nightdress. I read it in growing horror.

17 September. Night.

This is an exact record of what happened tonight. I feel as if I am dying.

I went to sleep quickly and was woken up by a flapping sound at the window. This has often happened since I walked on the cliffs at Whitby. Why isn't Dr Seward here? I heard a dog howling in the garden. I went to the window and caught sight of a huge bat. My mother, hearing my footsteps, came in to see me.

Suddenly, there was a loud crash at the window. Broken glass flew everywhere. I looked at the hole in the window – there was the head of a grey wolf. My mother screamed and tore at the flowers around my neck. Then she fell over.

I kept my eyes fixed on the window. The maids, hearing the noise, came in and laid my poor mother on the bed. I told them to have a drink of brandy. They went and never came back. I found them all drugged.

I am alone now, alone with the dead! I can hear the wolf howling through the broken window. What will happen to me? Goodbye, dear Arthur. I shall die tonight.

"What does it all mean?" I asked. "Was she mad?"

"Forget it for the moment," the Professor replied. "I will tell you later."

When Lucy woke up late in the afternoon, she looked around the room, shuddered and gave a loud cry. She wept weakly and silently for a long time.

19 SEPTEMBER

We watched Lucy all night, but she was too afraid to sleep. She was very weak in the morning. When she fell asleep at daylight, her open mouth showed pale gums drawn back from her teeth. Her teeth looked longer and sharper than usual. Later, she asked to see Arthur. He arrived at six o'clock, just as the sun was setting.

20 SEPTEMBER

Lucy was worse during the night and her teeth are even sharper and longer, especially the ones at the side in her top gum.

There was a full moonlight and I saw a bat flapping at the window pane. Lucy moved in her sleep and tore the garlic flowers from her throat. I replaced them. Whenever she awoke, she pressed the flowers to her face.

When the Professor came into the room at dawn and saw Lucy's face, he drew in his breath sharply. He leaned over and looked at her neck.

"The wounds on her throat have disappeared!" he whispered. "She is dying. It will not be long. Bring Arthur to see her."

When Arthur came into the room, Lucy opened her eyes and smiled lovingly at him. Suddenly, I heard her breathing become louder, her mouth opened and her pale gums drew back. Her teeth seemed to lengthen and sharpen. She spoke in a voice I had never heard before.

"Arthur, kiss me!" she murmured.

Arthur leaned over her. But Van Helsing, startled by Lucy's voice, pulled him back with both hands.

"No!" the Professor shouted. "No!"

A look of rage flickered across Lucy's face and her sharp teeth clamped together. Then she closed her eyes. Shortly afterwards, she opened them again and took hold of Van Helsing's hand.

"My true friend," she whispered. "Look after Arthur and give him peace!"

"I promise," the Professor whispered.

He turned to Arthur.

"Hold her hand," he said. "Now kiss her on the forehead, and only once."

Their eyes met instead of their lips. Then Lucy's eyes closed. Van Helsing took Arthur's arm and pulled him away.

"It's all over," he said. "She is dead."

So now I can finish this sad diary. I shall never begin another.

CHAPTER FIVE

Mina Harker's Journal: The Return of Count Dracula

22 SEPTEMBER

I was walking with Jonathan this morning in London, near Piccadilly, when I felt him clutch my arm tightly.

"My God!" he said under his breath.

I was very anxious. I always am now, ever since his illness earlier this year.

"What's wrong, my dear?" I asked.

His face was very pale and his eyes seemed to bulge in terror and amazement. He was staring at a tall, thin man with a large nose, black moustache and a pointed beard. This man was looking so closely at a pretty girl in the street that he did not see us.

I stared at the man, too, and shuddered. How cruel and hard his face was! His lips were bright red, his teeth a brilliant white and pointed like an animal's.

"What's wrong?" I asked again.

"Don't you know him?" Jonathan asked, his eyes never leaving the man's face.

"No, dear," I said gently. "Who is he?"

"It is the man himself," my husband whispered. "Here in Piccadilly."

He was obviously terrified.

"I believe it is Count Dracula!" he said, "but he has grown young. My God, if only I knew! Is it really him?"

We went a little further and sat in the park. Jonathan slept for about fifteen minutes and woke up quite cheerful again. He did not mention the stranger again. And I forgot about it when we arrived home, because there was bad news for us.

A telegram arrived from a stranger called Van Helsing, telling us that my dear, dear friend Lucy had died. And her mother, too. Such sorrow!

23 SEPTEMBER

Tonight I decided to read Jonathan's diary about the time he travelled to Transylvania. I was worried by his behaviour yesterday and I want to help him if I can.

Is it true? Or is it his imagination? Was he ill when he wrote all those terrible things? Only one part I know is the truth – Count Dracula was buying a house in London.

25 SEPTEMBER

Professor Van Helsing came to visit me today. What a strange meeting it was! My head is whirling round and round!

"I have read your letters to dear Miss Lucy," he said as he arrived. "Forgive me, but I have to know what happened to Miss Lucy in Whitby. Do you remember?"

"I wrote it all down," I told him. "You may read it if you wish."

I gave him my diary and he read it to the end in silence.

"This diary is like sunshine," he said at last, "it sheds light on a great deal. But the clouds roll in behind."

Later, I told him about the man Jonathan had seen in London and the horror he had felt.

"Please make my husband well again," I begged. "You may read the journal he kept in Transylvania if it will help."

Professor Van Helsing agreed. And when he had finished, he said what I had longed to hear ever since I had read about those terrible events.

"Strange and terrible," the Professor said, "but true!"

CHAPTER SIX

Dr Seward's Diary: The Terrible Truth

26 SEPTEMBER

It is only a week since I stopped writing my diary when dear Lucy died, but now I am starting it again! The Professor has told me something truly terrible this morning.

He turned up at my hospital and thrust a newspaper cutting under my nose.

The Westminster Gazette, 25 September

THE HAMPSTEAD HORROR

Another child has been found on Hampstead Heath this morning. It has the same tiny wound on the throat that the other children had.

"It is like the mark on poor Lucy's throat," I said sadly.

"What do you think that means?" the Professor asked. "Do you mean to say that you have no idea of the cause of Lucy's death, even after all the hints I have given you?"

"She died from loss of blood," I said.

"You are a clever man, John," my friend said, "but there are things that you cannot understand. That is the fault of science – it tries to explain everything."

"What are you saying?" I asked.

"Can you tell me why there are stories of vampire bats in South America that come at night and drink the blood of cattle and horses? Can you tell me why there are stories of sailors sleeping on deck at night who are sucked dry of blood?"

"Do you mean that Lucy was bitten by a vampire bat, here in London, in the nineteenth century?" I asked in amazement.

"I want you to believe in the things you cannot believe," Van Helsing said.

"You think that those small holes in the children's throats were made by the same thing that made the holes in Miss Lucy?" I asked.

"Alas, no, it is far worse," the Professor replied.

"In God's name, what do you mean?" I asked.

The Professor covered his face with his hands as he answered me.

"They were made by Miss Lucy!" he whispered.

I hit the table hard with my fist.

"Dr Van Helsing," I shouted, "are you mad?"

"I wish I was," he said. "It would be easier to bear than this. I have not told you before. I wanted to break it to you gently. I know how much you loved Miss Lucy, even hoped to marry her yourself before Arthur…"

"Forgive me," I said. "What are we going to do?"

The Professor took a key from his pocket and held it up.

"We are going to spend the night in the churchyard where Lucy lies. This is the key to her tomb. Then you will know that I speak the truth."

My heart sank. I knew that a terrible ordeal lay ahead of me.

We left for the churchyard at about ten o' clock that evening. We entered the family tomb by candlelight and came to Lucy's coffin. He lifted up the lid and I went nearer to look.

Lucy's coffin was empty.

CHAPTER SEVEN

Dr Seward's Diary: Death of a Vampire

27 SEPTEMBER

This afternoon, Van Helsing made me go back to Lucy's tomb. I stared down as he flung back the lid, afraid of what I might see. There lay Lucy, looking just as she had done on the day she had died.

"Is this a trick?" I gasped. "Why has her body not decayed? It is a week since she died!"

The Professor pulled back Lucy's lips to show her gleaming white teeth.

"They are even sharper than before," he said. "She can already bite little children."

I stood in silence, trembling.

"I must kill her," Van Helsing said simply.

I could not stop shaking.

"How?" I whispered.

"By driving a stake through her heart," he told me. "I shall need help, from you and Arthur, and his friend. We may have Count Dracula to deal with, too. He has the strength of twenty men. And he could call on his wolf to help."

"When?" I whispered.

"Tomorrow night at ten o' clock,"the Professor answered firmly.

28 SEPTEMBER

The four of us met this evening.

"What are we here for?" Arthur asked.

"I want you to come with me to the churchyard where Lucy is buried,"Van Helsing said gently.

"Why?" Arthur asked.

"To open her tomb!"Van Helsing told him.

Arthur's face turned deadly pale and he got up to leave.

"This is too much!" he said, shaking.

"Listen, please, I beg you!" the Professor said. "If Lucy is dead…"

"What do you mean?" Arthur asked angrily. "Has she been buried alive? Tell me, has she?"

"I did not say she was alive," Van Hesling said. "She is…"

"She is what?" Arthur shouted.

Van Helsing stood up.

"My dear fellow," he said, "it is my duty, to you and to everyone else to tell you. Your dear Lucy is now a vampire. She was bitten by a vampire called Count Dracula. Vampires never die. They add new victims by biting them. They spread their evil everywhere. Now Lucy is already biting children. If we can kill her, those children can still be saved. The marks on their throats will disappear. We must also set Lucy free."

I thought Arthur would faint in horror, but he followed us to that terrible place again. The night was dark, with gleams of moonlight from time to time. Inside the tomb, Arthur turned very pale when Lucy's coffin was opened and he saw that it was empty.

"Vampires can only move at night," the Professor said. "Wait with me outside and you will see stranger things than this empty coffin."

We stumbled outside into the fresh air and crouched in the dark without speaking. After a few minutes, we saw a white figure walking towards us. I heard Arthur gasp. It was his beloved Lucy! How changed she was! Her sweet face looked so cruel. Her lips were crimson with fresh blood, which trickled down her chin onto her white robe. We shuddered with horror. If I had not held Arthur's arm, he would have fainted.

We stepped out and stood in front of the door to the tomb. When Lucy saw us, she stepped back angrily, her eyes full of evil.

"Come with me, Arthur," she whispered sweetly. "Come with me! Leave the others."

Arthur moved towards her, his arms open, as if he

were in a trance. Van Helsing ran forward and held a small crucifix between them. Lucy ran away towards the tomb and stood for a moment, looking at us as if she wanted to kill us all.

"Arthur, shall I do what I said?" Van Helsing shouted. "Tell me now, there isn't much time!"

Arthur threw himself to his knees and hid his face in his hands.

"Do what you must, friend," he cried. "There can be no horror greater than this!"

But as he spoke, we saw Lucy's body pass through the wall into the tomb.

"We shall have to finish our work tomorrow," Van Helsing said.

29 SEPTEMBER

It is over! Lucy is at peace once again. We killed her after she had returned to her coffin. Her face became that of Lucy again, sweet and pure and gentle. Arthur kissed her before we left.

But one task still remains – to kill Count Dracula.

CHAPTER EIGHT

Mina Harker's Journal: The Hunt for Count Dracula

30 SEPTEMBER

We are next to the vampire's hiding-place!

It had already become clear to us all that Count Dracula must be hiding in the house he had bought in London. Jonathan checked all the details – the Count's cargo of fifty boxes was delivered to that house, safely taken from the Russian ship after the big storm at Whitby. To our amazement, that house is next to Dr Seward's hospital.

We are all here now: myself, Jonathan, Arthur, his friend and Professor Van Helsing.

"I think I should tell you something about the kind of enemy we are looking for," the Professor said. He stared at us for a while. "If I had known then what I have found out now about vampires, we might have saved Miss Lucy. The vampire grows stronger as he feeds on our blood. Then he has more power to do evil. Count Dracula is as strong as twenty men. He is cunning. He can appear wherever he wants, in whatever shape he chooses. By day, he can appear in the shape of a man. He has power over the storm, the fog, the thunder. Animals obey him. He can grow, he can become smaller, or he can vanish."

The Professor sighed deeply.

"It will be a terrible task to hunt him down," he said at last. "Will you help me?"

We all nodded.

"We have some advantage over Count Dracula," the Professor said. "We have scientific knowledge. We are free to act and to think. And, most important of all, we have the night and the day for our work. We know that a stake through the heart will kill him. Garlic, wild roses and the crucifix will all stop him from moving. We must destroy all the boxes he brought from Transylvania."

"Why?" we asked together.

"They are his home during the day," the Professor said.

They have just left for Count Dracula's house. I admit that I was too afraid to go with them. I was also too anxious to sleep. I heard dogs barking outside and went to the window. All was dark and silent out there, except for a thin streak of white mist creeping across the grass to the house.

I am going to pull the bedclothes over my head and try to sleep.

1 OCTOBER

I had a very strange dream last night. A white mist seeped through the cracks of my bedroom door. It got thicker and thicker, and a red light, like an eye, seemed to shine from it. This light divided and shone like two red eyes, like the ones poor Lucy had talked about at Whitby.

I remembered those awful women that Jonathan had seen in the white mist at Castle Dracula, and I felt faint with horror. Just before I fainted, I saw a ghastly white face bending over me.

I must ask Dr Seward to give me something to help me sleep.

CHAPTER NINE

Dr Seward's Diary: Count Dracula Strikes Again

1 OCTOBER

We entered Count Dracula's house at nearly five o'clock this morning. The place was alive with rats! Out of fifty boxes, we found only twenty-nine in the house.

3 OCTOBER

A terrible thing has happened. It is only thanks to one of my own patients in the hospital that it was not worse. My patient told me that he had seen a man with red eyes, a man who had laughed and said that he was waiting for Mina Harker!

I told Professor Van Helsing at once and we broke open the door of the Harkers' bedroom.

What I saw in that room appalled me. My heart seemed to stop beating, and the bristles rose on the back of my neck. In the bright moonlight, I saw Jonathan Harker, breathing heavily, his eyes closed. Kneeling next to the bed was Mina. By her side stood Count Dracula. His right hand was forcing Mina's face down on his chest. The front of her nightdress was smeared with blood, and blood trickled down the Count's chest.

As we burst into the room,
Count Dracula turned
to look at us. His eyes
flamed red and his white
sharp teeth clamped
together like those of
a wild beast. He flung
Mina onto the bed and
sprang at us. We lifted
up our crucifixes and
walked forward. A thin white smoke crept under
the door and he disappeared. Then we saw a bat…

Mrs Harker gave a piercing scream and
lay helpless. Blood smeared her lips and
cheeks and chin. A thin stream of blood trickled
from her throat and her eyes were mad with terror. She
put her hands over her face and wept with despair.

Poor Mr Harker was in a terrible state for the rest of
the day. I could see that Mina's lips were drawn back
slightly over her teeth, like poor Lucy's, but I did not say
anything to her husband. There were no signs that her
teeth were growing sharper, but I feared that this might
happen later. I also feared that if Mina became a vampire,
she would not be alone. I am sure that Jonathan would
follow her into that terrible unknown land.

During the afternoon, we broke into another house in Piccadilly where we hoped to find the last boxes of the cargo. They were all there — except for one! The house smelled vile, just like the house next to Dr Seward's, and we knew that Count Dracula must have been there.

Suddenly, we heard slow, careful footsteps in the hall. Then, with a single jump, Count Dracula leapt into the room where we were standing. As he saw us, a snarl passed over his face, showing long, pointed teeth. I held up my crucifix and walked forward. The Count's face became greenish-yellow as he stepped back angrily. Then he threw himself through the window. He jumped up from the ground in the light of the setting sun and called up to us.

"You shall be sorry, each one of you! My revenge has just begun!"

"We must do all we can to find the last box," Van Helsing whispered. "If we do not, the Count could lie hidden from us for years."

We took it in turns to guard Mina this evening.

4 OCTOBER

At about four o' clock this morning, Mrs Harker asked me to fetch Professor Van Helsing.

"Is anything wrong?" I asked, alarmed.

"No," she replied, "but bring him now. I have an idea."

A few minutes later, Van Helsing appeared.

"I want you to hypnotise me, Professor!" Mrs Harker said cheerfully. "Do it before dawn! I feel I can tell you where the Count is. Do it now!"

The Professor did as she asked. Mina stared with a faraway look in her eyes.

"Where are you?" the Professor whispered.

"I do not know! It is all strange to me," Mina replied. "It is dark."

"What do you hear?" the Professor asked.

"The lapping of the water," Mrs Harker replied. "I am on a ship. I am sleeping."

When Mrs Harker had awoken from her trance, Professor Van Helsing looked at us all calmly.

"Count Dracula has taken his last earth-box on board ship," he said. "He thinks he will escape us."

"Why not let him go?" Mrs Harker asked.

The Professor's face became serious.

"We must find him," he said, "we must! Time is our enemy now. Once he has bitten you, there will be no stopping his power over you – except by his death."

As we listened in horror, I managed to catch Mina Harker as she fainted.

CHAPTER TEN

Mina Harker's Journal: The Death of Count Dracula

15 OCTOBER

We left England today, travelling overland.

I am not sleeping well and the Professor hypnotises me between sunset and sunrise.

30 OCTOBER

Arthur and my dear Jonathan will make their way to Castle Dracula by steamer. Dr Seward and Arthur's friend will ride along the banks of the river. Professor Van Helsing and I will travel overland, the same way that Jonathan travelled in May.

Jonathan was angry with the Professor.

"Do you mean to say, Professor Helsing," he shouted, "that you want to take Mina, tainted as she is with the devil's illness, right into the jaws of his death-trap? No, I shall not allow it!"

He paused for a moment, unable to speak.

"You have not seen that awful place," he whispered at last. "Have you felt the vampire's lips upon your throat? What have we done to deserve such terror?"

My poor husband collapsed on the sofa. But the Professor calmed us all.

"Oh, my friend," he said gently, "it is because I want to save your wife that we are going to that terrible place. If the Count escapes us this time, he may sleep in his castle for a century, and in time, dear Mina will become a vampire."

He looked at my husband.

"She would be like those other women you saw there, Jonathan. Do you remember them? Yes, I see you shudder as I speak."

"Do what you must," my husband sobbed. "We are in the hands of God!"

Later – I have said good-bye to my darling husband. We may never meet again. Courage, Mina!

2 NOVEMBER

Van Helsing hypnotised me this morning. He says that I answered, "Darkness, creaking wood and roaring water," so it seems that the river is going into the mountains. I hope that my darling husband is not in danger.

4 NOVEMBER

It is so cold. The grey heavy sky is full of snow, and if it falls, it will stay all winter. I sleep most of the time. I have lost all my appetite. The Professor has tried to hypnotise me, but he has had no effect.

We are climbing higher and higher into the mountains. I remember the way from Jonathan's journal. I sleep less.

5 NOVEMBER

This has been a day of horror. We both felt nervous all day long. I was wide awake and could not eat anything. After dark, the Professor was so afraid that he lit a fire and put a ring of wild roses and garlic around me. I was terrified and clung to his arm.

The Professor told me what happened next.

"Even in the dark, I could see a faint white light in the distance," he said. "It hovered above the snow and seemed to take the shape of three women. I thought my imagination was playing tricks on me, that I was simply remembering what your dear husband described in his journal. Then the horses started to scream. The white figures came closer and formed a circle around you, dear Mina. But you sat quite calm, whispering, "It is safe here inside the circle!" The women now stood before us. "Come, sister, come with us," they whispered sweetly. I picked up a piece of blazing firewood and held up my crucifix until dawn. Those terrible figures melted away."

I was horrified when the Professor finished his story.

"Let us go from this awful place!" I cried.

6 NOVEMBER

We travelled all day until we saw the outline of Castle Dracula in the distance. There it sat, perched on the edge of a steep precipice, a thousand feet on the top of a hill. We heard wolves howling across the snow. Below us lay the river.

Suddenly, straight in front of us, we saw it – a cart carrying an enormous wooden box, rushing towards Castle Dracula. My heart leapt with joy.

"It is nearly over," the Professor whispered. "But it is getting dark. We must kill Count Dracula before he can take any shape he chooses and escape us forever."

I looked through the eye-glass.

"I can see the others!" I called in excitement, "they're closing in on the cart! We must help them!"

But the snow began to whirl more thickly around us, blotting everyone from our sight. The wolves started to howl again, and I could see them gathering in groups of twos and threes. I took out my revolver.

We waited. The wind came in fierce bursts, driving the snow over us. We could see nothing beyond us. Later, the wind changed direction and started to blow the snow away from us. Now we could see everybody, coming closer and closer. The Professor and I moved forward at last, and crouched down behind a rock, guns ready.

Then I heard my husband's voice.

"STOP!" he shouted.

At the same time, Van Helsing and I stood up and pointed our weapons at the men on the cart. Seeing that they were surrounded, they stopped the horses and formed a circle. Jonathan reached the circle first and forced his way through.

"Hurry, hurry!" I whispered, "the sun's setting!"

Jonathan jumped onto the cart. I held my breath, hardly daring to watch. With a strength I did not know he possessed, my dear husband pushed the great box onto the ground. Then he jumped from the cart and desperately attacked the box with his knife.

Suddenly, the lid of the box flew open.

I leaned forward and stared down into the box. Count Dracula was lying there, deathly pale like a wax figure. His red eyes glared with the evil look I knew so well. As he looked at the setting sun, that look turned to one of triumph.

Suddenly, I saw the flash of Jonathan's great knife as he raised it high and plunged it into the Count's body. It was a miracle. As we watched, Count Dracula crumbled into dust and disappeared forever from our sight.

But in his last moment, I was glad to see a look of peace on his face.